This book is a gift from:

Believe in Books
Literacy Foundation

"Supporting literacy initiatives
throughout New England"

This book belongs to:

_____

www.believeinbooks.org

THE PENNY

THE PENNY

written by ANDY CUTTS

illustrated by KATHERINE ROY

ISBN 978-0-615-45834-2

Text copyright © 2011 Andy Cutts
Illustrations copyright © 2011 Katherine Roy

Book and jacket design by Katherine Roy
Printed and bound in New Hampshire

www.readthepenny.com

For Andrea

Thanks to the many friends and family who helped and guided.

Six-year-old Annie stood silently nearby as her father finished cutting the old wooden sailboat into pieces. Different shapes and sizes of wood, some still painted bright blue, lay scattered on the ground.

Holding his saw, her father picked up the largest remaining piece—the prow of the old boat. Instead of cutting it apart, he nestled it under a nearby willow tree.

Tucking her into bed that night, Annie's father was quiet.

"Why were you so sad today, Daddy?" Annie asked, sitting up in bed. Then, wanting to cheer him up, she added, "Can you tell me a story about the boat?"

Her father smiled. He thought for a few moments, nodded to her, then began slowly… "There once was a man named Peter Pennyworth. His grandkids called him 'Grampete.' He and his wife Dorrie owned a little cottage on a big lake called Winnipesaukee.

Their family found plenty to do at the lake. They swam; they fished. They paddled their old canvas canoe. But for Grampete the days at the cottage still weren't complete. When the wind blew and the wave-tops turned white, he wanted to sail. Grampete didn't have enough money to buy a sailboat. But he was good with his hands, so he decided to build one himself.

He had never built a boat like this. He wanted it to be safe in the shifting winds and surprise storms of the big lake. Twice he drew up plans for the boat, but each time he realized they weren't quite right.

So he started over. When he was finally satisfied, Grampete picked the proper piece of wood for each curve of the boat's hull.

After working for almost a year, he stood back to admire what he had done. His new sailboat was finished. Her tall mast was made from an Alaskan fir tree. She was painted bright blue. Dorrie named her 'Penny.'

The next spring Grampete gathered the neighbors to help launch Penny. Everyone wanted to watch the beautiful blue wooden boat take her first sail.

Six strong men slowly slid her down the dock and into the water. Penny was finally floating! Smiling broadly, Mr. Grandy, a big quiet man from a cottage nearby, slapped Grampete heartily on the back.

For the next several summers Penny waltzed
the wave-tops of Lake Winnipesaukee.

One day Mr. Grandy and Grampete set off in Penny for an afternoon sail. Mr. Grandy was holding the tiller when the Mount Washington rounded Diamond Island, heading their way. 'The Mount', as Grampete called her, was a passenger steamer—well over a hundred feet long. Every day she traveled around the lake on a sightseeing tour.

Grampete saw that the boats were too close. He knew that a fast ship such as the Mount couldn't turn quickly. If Penny didn't change course, she could be smashed to pieces!

'Ready about; hard a' lee!' shouted Mr. Grandy. He yanked hard on the tiller and Grampete ducked his head as the mainsail swung across the boat. Penny turned clear of the Mount just in time.

Grampete gave a low whistle. 'Whew, that was close,' he gasped, winking at Mr. Grandy. 'We almost went for a very long swim!'

A few nights later Grampete was wakened by the sound of loud banging on the back door. It was dark, the wind was howling, and from his bed he heard waves smashing against the shore. Hurrying downstairs, he opened the door. Mr. Grandy stood there with a frightful look on his face.

'Penny broke free from her mooring,' Mr. Grandy exclaimed, 'She's crashing on the rocks!'

Grampete threw on a rain slicker and headed into the heavy wind. Mr. Grandy was ahead, bravely wading into the churning waves toward the boat.

The two men tried desperately to keep Penny off the rocks. As the sun came up, more men arrived to help lift the splintered sailboat up onto the shore.

Exhausted, the men stood around her looking at the damage. Penny's hull was crushed and her mast cracked. Grampete stood silently by the wreck, tears in his eyes.

Penny's mooring was empty for the next few years. Grampete didn't rebuild her right away. The sight of his broken boat in the basement left him feeling empty. But he found other ways to keep busy.

On sunny days he worked in the yard. On stormy days he practiced his cello or, sitting at the piano, he wrote children's songs. On very special nights he sang for his grandkids while playing songs on a banjo he had made from a cookie tin.

Still, he missed Penny. And so, during one long winter,
he carefully pieced her back together again.

Years passed. One day Grampete's young grandson asked if he could sail Penny alone. Grampete gave him permission but warned him to stay in the shelter of the cove. He also reminded him to watch the weather. If the wind picked up, he was to return in a hurry.

To practice steering with the tiller, the boy launched a life ring far from the boat and then steered carefully to pick it up. This was a great game, and he played it again and again for more than an hour. He was so busy chasing the ring that he didn't realize he had sailed past the point of the cove, losing sight of the cottage. He also didn't notice that the wind had picked up.

When Grampete didn't see Penny's sail, he grew worried. Storm clouds had gathered over the lake. He had to find Penny and his grandson. By the time he launched the old red canvas canoe, a wild wind had turned the waves into whitecaps.

With its flat bottom, the canoe rolled dangerously in the storm. To steer, Grampete knelt low in the bow and paddled hard. He struggled against the strong waves as the canoe pounded from one crest to another.

In the sailboat the boy suddenly realized the danger when a wave spilled over Penny's side. Then he heard a shout above the wind and, turning toward the sound, saw his grandfather straining not to swamp the canoe. Penny was built for bad weather, but the canoe was not!"

Annie's father stopped the story. "Do you know who the grandson in the story was, Annie?" he asked.

"Was it you, Daddy?" she replied.

"Yes, I was twelve years old," he said, softly. "Seeing the storm had made me too scared to think. Grampete's voice nearby calmed me down. He instructed me to lower the sail. When I did that, I could control the boat. I grew brave enough to sail it back home, all by myself."

Then, winking toward her he laughed, "Boy, was I in trouble when Grampete finally landed the canoe!"

They were both very quiet for a few moments, and then Annie's dad spoke again.

"The next November Grampete passed away. Penny sailed for many more years, but often needed repairs. Her blue paint had peeled. Some of her wood became soft and spongy. A long crack appeared in her hull. It was my turn to fix her, but the job seemed too big. The longer she sat broken in the yard, the worse I felt about it. It hurt my heart," he sighed, "but finally I realized it was time to let her go."

"Maybe we could make something new from Penny's pieces," Annie suggested.

Her dad broke into a big smile. "Annie," he responded, "that's a great idea. Grampete would have liked that very much." And with that he kissed her on the forehead, turned off the light, and closed her bedroom door behind him.